*For Dad, who taught me
how to get my hooves dirty*

ORCHARD BOOKS

First published in 2014 in the United States by Little, Brown and Company
This edition published in 2015 by The Watts Publishing Group

9 10

A CIP catalogue record for this book is available from the British Library.

ISBN 978 1 40833 695 3

Printed and bound in Great Britain by CPI Group (UK) Ltd, Croydon, CR0 4YY

MIX
Paper from
responsible sources
FSC® C104740
www.fsc.org

The paper and board used in this book are made from wood from responsible sources

Orchard Books
An imprint of Hachette Children's Group
Part of The Watts Publishing Group Limited
Carmelite House, 50 Victoria Embankment, London EC4Y 0DZ

An Hachette UK Company
www.hachette.co.uk
www.hachettechildrens.co.uk

Applejack

* * and * *

The Secret Diary Switcheroo

Written by G. M. Berrow

ORCHARD

Contents

✶ ✶ ✶

CHAPTER 1

The Pie-Eatin' Extravaganza

"Thirty seconds left, y'all!" Applejack hollered into a megaphone. "Better hurry up an' eat yer treats!" At the sound of her voice, the contestants of the pie-eating contest all pushed harder to finish their pies. Pinkie Pie squealed gleefully and shoved another piece into her mouth with ease. A glob of sauce dripped onto her bib, which read PIE IS MY NAME. Next to her, little Scootaloo attempted in vain to munch on a second piece. She stopped mid-bite, held her tummy, and groaned. Minty and Lyra were in a similar state, only each halfway through a pie. But down at the end of the row, something interesting was happening.

Applejack couldn't believe her eyes. The clock had only twenty-five seconds left on it, but the most unlikely pony of all – well, technically he was a *donkey* – was in the lead to win the Seventh Annual Sweet Apple Acres Pie-Eatin' Extravaganza! Cranky Doodle Donkey usually liked to spend his days inside his cottage on the outskirts of Ponyville, minding his own business. But something about eatin' these pies must've cranked his gears, because there he was, shovelling them into his gob with the best of them.

"You can do it, Lyra!" shouted Sweetie Drops from the audience. She waved a homemade flag sewn with a picture of Lyra's cutie mark – a golden lyre. Lyra smiled and waved back, mouth full. The two ponies were best buddies.

Next in line was Mayor Mare. She was usually one of the most proper ponies in town. She was an authority figure, so she liked to remain composed.

But right now, she was attempting to hold her own against Cranky. Her approach was unique. She took methodical, dainty bites and wiped her mouth after each one. She kept saying things like "Oh my!" and "Delicious!" and "I couldn't possibly!"

The seconds ticked down on the timer. Everypony leaned in. It was now pretty much a race between Pinkie Pie, Mayor Mare, and Cranky Doodle Donkey. Minty, Lyra, and Scootaloo gave up and started cheering along with the crowd.

"Ten! Nine! Eight!" the ponies shouted. "Seven! Six! Five!" Applejack trotted over to the three finalists. Pinkie Pie stopped and let out a loud burp, then giggled. The race was now between Cranky and the mayor. "Four! Three! Two!" All of a sudden, Cranky grunted and swallowed two more pieces of pie.

"And … ONE!" Applejack shouted. "Put the pies down, everypony!"

Applejack gave both Cranky and Mayor Mare an encouraging wink. Of all the ponies in Ponyville, she never thought it would be down to these two. She and her friends Princess Twilight Sparkle, Fluttershy, Pinkie Pie, Rainbow Dash, and Rarity had all thought one of the big stallions in town would win. But Big McIntosh, Senior Mint, Overhaul, and Snowflake had all decided to sit it out this year to give somepony else a chance.

"The winner of the Sweet Apple Acres Pie-Eatin' Extravaganza is…" Applejack stepped forward on the wooden platform stage. "Cranky Doodle Donkey!" The crowd erupted in cheers, and Mayor Mare nodded in approval at her competition.

Apple Bloom placed a crown of apples on Cranky's head. He gave the filly a tiny smile, then immediately reverted to his trademark frown. Applejack turned to the crowd and held the megaphone up to her mouth. "It sure was a close one, folks! Let's give all our pie eaters a round o' applause!"

The ponies stomped their hooves on the dirt and cheered. *It's real nice to see the underdog win,* thought Applejack. *Or, in this case, an underdonkey.* Either way, the pie-eating contest was much more exciting than in previous years. Applejack couldn't help but feel like it was one for the books.

CHAPTER 2

A Sweet Proposal

"Is this over yet?" Cranky growled, ripping the crown off his prickly head. He was, after all, called "Cranky" for a reason. "I have things to do! I can't just hang around all day, you know."

"Of course, champ." Applejack smirked. She patted him on the back.

"Great job today." He grunted and looked at her hoof as if he couldn't believe she'd touched him.

Matilda, his lady love, walked up to greet them. "You won! I'm so proud," she said with a smile. Applejack noticed a slight blush on Cranky's face.

"Enough with the compliments! I just ate some pie," he grumbled.

"But you did it super-de-dooper awesomeriffically!" Pinkie called out as she bounded over. She was still wearing her bib. She didn't look at all upset that she'd lost. "You should be proud of yourself, too!"

"Way to go, Cranky!" said Twilight Sparkle as she, Rarity, Fluttershy, and Rainbow Dash joined them.

Applejack could sense how uncomfortable Cranky was getting.

"All right, y'all. Give the champion his space." She motioned for the ponies to step back. Cranky and Matilda nodded gratefully. As the two donkeys turned toward home, Applejack thought about how a pony never really knows what to expect from others. They sure could surprise ya!

Applejack had learned an important lesson today. And she didn't want to forget it. "Heya, Twilight," Applejack said. "Who has our journal? I haven't written an entry in a long time, but I think I got somethin' to say about Cranky."

Recently, the six ponies had been so tied up with other activities that they hadn't been writing in the journal they shared. Originally, they'd modelled it after the *Journal of the Two Sisters* that Princess Celestia and Princess Luna shared. But now it had become so much more than that to the friends. It was high time that one of them paid it a little attention. And that pony was going to be Applejack.

"Great idea!" Twilight grinned. She was always trying to get the others to participate in recording their lessons.

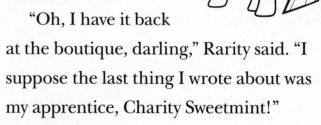

"Oh, I have it back at the boutique, darling," Rarity said. "I suppose the last thing I wrote about was my apprentice, Charity Sweetmint!"

"Whoo-ee! That pony sure was a hoof-ful." Applejack nodded, recalling how the young fashionista had tried to become just like Rarity. "But she sure meant well, of course."

"Of course she did!" Rarity nodded, and her perfectly coiffed purple mane  swayed gently. "And you'll all be thrilled to hear that she's doing fabulously with her own line in Manehattan. She's being featured as a 'Designer to Watch' in *PegasUs Weekly*!"

"That's great news! So I'll come on by and grab the journal now, if that's all right with you, Rarity," Applejack said. "Just got to clean up this mess, and I'll be right over."

"I'll help!" Pinkie Pie squeaked. "By taking some of those scrum-dilly-umptious leftover pies off your hooves…" She patted her already bulging tummy. How she could eat any *more* pie after the contest was beyond Applejack. As Granny Smith would say, Pinkie Pie must have a "hollow hoof" where she was hiding all that food!

"I think somepony already beat ya to it," Applejack said. She pointed to the table. Apple Bloom and Sweetie Belle were already "helping" by chowing down and making an even bigger mess. The six ponies all chuckled.

"Excuse me, ladies. I don't mean to interrupt," said a beige-colored stallion with a light blue mane as he trotted up to the group. His cutie mark was a blue ribbon. A quick series of looks exchanged among the friends made it clear that nopony recognized him. "But are you Applejack of Sweet Apple Acres?" he asked, raising an eyebrow.

"Yep, that's me." Applejack tipped her hat. "What can I do for ya?"

"My name is Blue Ribbon. I run the

Best of Equestria Awards," said the stallion. He passed Applejack a business card. Sure as the sun sits in the sky, it said:

Blue Ribbon
Best of Equestria Awards

Finding the Best Businesses in Equestria
Since the First Summer Sun Celebration

"I'm here to tell you that Sweet Apple Acres has been named as a finalist in our Best Orchard in Equestria contest!"

"Really?" Applejack exclaimed.

"I mean, thank ya kindly, Mr. Ribbon."
She looked to her friends, who had all
started whispering excitedly to one
another. "Is there anything I need to do
for ya?"

"Not too much . . ." Blue Ribbon
smiled. He flipped open a folder filled
with forms. He scanned the page with his
hoof and jotted down some notes. "We'll
come by the farm on Friday to check out
the place. If the harvest numbers you've
reported to the *Equestria Farmers' Almanac*
are correct, you've got nothing to worry
about. That's some apple yield! I've never
seen anything like it in all my years."

"Well, we do try our best over at Sweet
Apple Acres." Applejack tried to recall the
numbers they'd reported to the almanac.
Applejack tipped her hat at Blue Ribbon.
"We'll be ready, sir."

"I hope so," Blue Ribbon said, putting his hoof on her shoulder. "The winner of the award will be named the official apple supplier for Canterlot Castle."

"How divine!" Rarity gasped. "Does it include VIP access to all the events? For Applejack *and* her friends?"

"To the Wonderbolts Derby?!" said Rainbow Dash. "Because that's the only one I really care about."

Applejack shot her friends a look to shush them, but Rarity had a dreamy look in her eyes and Rainbow Dash had already stopped paying attention.

"There will be lots of special perks," Blue Ribbon said. "Front-row seats at the Equestria Rodeo definitely. Tickets to the Hearth's Warming Eve Annual Ball. Oh, and one grand prize that is sure to delight any farmpony..."

"That all sounds real nice, Mr. Ribbon," Applejack replied. "But we Apples don't need any prizes—"

"What about a brand-new plot of land?" Blue Ribbon smirked.

Applejack's jaw dropped in surprise. Now that really *was* a prize worth winnin'! She tried to hide her elation.

"See you on Friday, Applejack." Blue Ribbon turned on his hoof and began to walk away. "Good luck!"

If Applejack had anything to say about it, she wouldn't need a smidgen of luck. Just good old-fashioned hard work.

"Hey, Applejack," said Twilight Sparkle. "How about the five of us help you out this applebuck season?"

CHAPTER 3

The Big Announcement

Applejack scribbled in the journal and dotted the end of her sentence happily. The entry was about Cranky Doodle Donkey, the pie-eating contest, and how you never really know what to expect of ponies (or donkeys):

Today, I learned that sometimes even those

friends with a hitch in their giddyup like Cranky Doodle Donkey like to be included from time to time. And you never know – they might just take the whole darn tootin' cake! (Or pie.)

Applejack thought her hoofwriting looked a little like chicken scratch, but all in all it wasn't bad. She felt a wave of satisfaction wash over her. The feeling was almost as good as when she sat down to dinner each night after a long, strenuous day of applebucking.

After the contest, there was one more big surprise! Sweet Apple Acres is up for an award for Best Orchard in Equestria. It's mighty excitin', and my friends and I plan to get the farm ready together. They each volunteered to help me for a day this week. Now all that's left is to tell the rest of the Apple family at supper. Well, that and all the hard work!

"Applejack!" a voice called.

Applejack slammed the journal shut and hollered, "I'm comin', Granny!"

On her way out the door, Applejack grabbed her brown cowgirl hat from its peg by the door and threw it atop her head. She never liked to go anywhere without it – even if it was just to another room in the house. There were extras in the hats-and-bows closet, but this one was the best. It was perfectly broken in.

Applejack trotted down the hallway, following the scent of something delicious. Sure enough, her nose led her straight to the kitchen. Granny Smith stood at the stove, stirring a bubbling pot of food.

"Were you busy, sugarcube?" Granny Smith asked without turning around. "I just thought you wouldn't mind helping yer old granny set the table fer dinner."

"Of course I don't mind!" Applejack

replied. She crossed over to the cabinet and started pulling down some bright green dishes. The smell from the pot wafted over. She inhaled deeply. "What're we havin'? My tummy is rumbling just from the yummy smell."

"Your favorite – carrot stew." Granny nodded with a knowing smile. "I figured you could use a hearty meal after all the work you put in today with the contest. I sure hope ya can find some time to rest this week."

"I doubt it!" Applejack said as she carried the dishes and napkins over to the table. She was starting to get real excited to tell her family about the award.

Applejack imagined the big blue

ribbon they'd get to hang on the Sweet Apple Acres sign. She kept on daydreaming as she set the four place settings – one for each member of the Apple family.

They always sat in the same spots. Applejack and Big Mac sat on the far ends with Granny and Apple Bloom across from each other in the middle. It started out that way when Apple Bloom was just knee-high to a pig's eye.

"Say, I don't suppose you know where my sister and brother are, do ya?" Applejack peered out the front window. She just saw the normal view of the farmyard – rolling green hills, a white picket fence, and ... no Apple Bloom or Big Mac in sight. Applejack's stomach gave another loud rumble.

"I'm sure they'll be along in a minute

or two, honeycrisp. You should sit down and eat while the gettin's good." Granny carried the pot over to the table and placed it on the table. She took a ladle, scooped some of the orange-colored broth into a bowl, and tried to pass it to Applejack. Tantalizing, fragrant swirls of steam billowed up.

Applejack shook her head in protest. "I'm mighty hungry, but I don't want to start eating without them." It was a tradition for the Apple family to eat dinner together every night, and everypony knew that the Apples cared about tradition. Why, Sweet Apple Acres was practically built on it! That and a sturdy foundation of hoof-chopped lumber, of course. "We'll wait," said Applejack, taking her seat at the wooden farm table. "Let's just chat for a bit until they get on home."

"Whatever you say!" Granny raised her hooves in the air in surrender. "Applejack,

you sure can be more stubborn than an old cow on a new harness," Granny said, taking a seat. "So what were ya gettin' up to when I called ya down?"

Applejack smiled. She wanted to tell Granny about the award, but she knew the effect would be much better if she waited 'til the whole gang was there. "Well, I was writing in this journal that I have with my friends. I forgot how good it feels to put somethin' down on paper…"

✷ ✴ ✴

 **23**

Twenty minutes later, the stew had gone completely cold. Applejack was annoyed at first, but now she was just plum worried. What if Apple Bloom had somehow fallen into a sinkhole and Big Mac was strugglin' to rescue her all on his own? Or what if Big Mac had accidentally sniffed a giant funflower – the only plant he's allergic to? Why, he could be swollen up like one of Pinkie Pie's balloons! Or what if—

"Sorry to interrupt yer deep ponderin', dear, but I'm sure Apple Bloom and Big Mac are just fine! They'll have a reason for bein' late," Granny said.

Applejack frowned and cocked her head to the side. She hadn't even said any of that out loud! "Well, whatever the reason is, I hope it's good," she said.

Chapter 4

A Chilly Stew Reception

Applejack looked at her siblings sternly.
She wasn't about to let this sort of
behavior slide. "Well? Tell me why y'all
were so late to supper!" She walked
around them like a royal guard drill
sergeant. Big Mac shrugged. Apple
Bloom looked down at the ground in

shame. "I was worried sick about y'all!"

"Sorry, Applejack, it's all my fault. After the contest, I asked Big Mac to help fix some broken floorboards in the Cutie Mark Crusaders' clubhouse."

Big Mac nodded. "Eeyup."

Applejack raised an eyebrow. "And that took all evening?"

"Well…no…after that, the Cutie Mark Crusaders were supposed to have an Alicorn tea party – we all wear wings and horns and pretend we are the four princesses of Equestria," Apple Bloom said excitedly. "I was being Princess Luna! See?" She pointed her hoof at her fake horn and wings, fashioned out of dark blue card. They were lopsided and strapped on with some string. "And we needed somepony to be Princess Cadance and Big Mac was there, so we asked him if he would and he said—"

"Eeyup." Big Mac shrugged with a sheepish smile and turned to show Applejack his pink paper wings.

Applejack gave them another stern look. "I'm glad you two had fun, but was it really fair to make Granny wait to eat dinner?" She gestured to Granny, who looked completely content.

"Really, I'm fine, sugarcube," Granny said, but Applejack didn't even hear her. It was hard to stop the Applejack train once it left the station.

Apple Bloom whimpered. "But, Applejack! I didn't mean to—"

"Say you're sorry, Apple Bloom,"

Applejack insisted. Big Mac and Granny Smith exchanged a concerned look. Sometimes Applejack got too carried away with her "family rules."

Apple Bloom raised her eyebrows and forced the words out, trying to lay it on  thick. "I'm reeeeal sorry, Granny."

"Good. Now let's eat." Applejack looked satisfied. "I have somethin' exciting to tell all of ya!" The ponies took their seats as Granny reheated the stew. Was it Applejack's imagination or did her family all seem annoyed with her? Maybe the spicy carrot concoction was just what they all needed to warm up the chilliness in the room.

Oh well, Applejack thought. *Somepony has to be in charge around here.* If she didn't hold this family together, it would fall apart. Applejack took a large gulp of stew. "Do y'all want to hear my news or not?"

After dinner, Applejack decided it was still a bit too early to hit the hay. But which task from her long to-do list to complete? She had just settled on going to the barn to prep the wagons for tomorrow's work in the orchard when Granny pulled her aside.

Applejack fidgeted. "What is it? I'm mighty busy right now." She'd had enough of dilly-dallying. It was time to get her hooves dirty – at least a little bit before she called it a night. She pictured the Best of Equestria blue ribbon emblem that would be stamped on all their apple crates after they won the award. It was going to look five ways from fancy!

"Just follow me, dear." Granny started up the creaky wooden stairs toward the farmhouse attic. "I got somethin' I have a mind to show ya."

Applejack hated the attic. It gave her the heebie-jeebies, the hootie-jooties, and even the humble-jumbles. "I'll just wait down here, thanks."

"Whatever suits ya." Granny chuckled and slowly climbed the rest of the stairs. She pulled the creaky attic door. Her head disappeared into the dark void, but her hooves remained on the top step. It reminded Applejack of the campfire story Rainbow Dash had told on their camping trip about the Headless Horse. Applejack shuddered.

"Nothin' to be afraid of up here but a

whole lotta apple crates and cobwebs!"
Granny Smith's voice was muffled. "Now
where did I put that ole'…?" She threw
an old, moth-eaten knit blanket down the
stairs, and it landed on Applejack's head.
She swiped it away, and several broken
fiddles tumbled down. "Fiddle-faddle!"
said Granny in frustration. "I just know
it's up here somewhere." An old pony doll
tumbled out and landed on one of the
fiddles. It gave a weak twang.

"Do ya need help?" Applejack asked.
She craned to see what Granny was
moving around up there, but it was too
dark. "Was it a toy pony?" Applejack
picked up the old pony doll, and a wave of
nostalgia washed over her. The cowpony
wore a hat like hers – except his was
bright green. His coat was red, and his
mane was dark brown. He had a lasso

cutie mark. It was her toy from when she was just a little filly! She'd named him Yeehaw. Back then, she'd carried him everywhere with her – playing on the farm, pretending to be cowponies. Yeehaw looked a little worse for the wear now. *I wonder*... thought Applejack. She lifted up his back left boot. Sure enough, the inscription was still there: *A.J.*

Applejack set the doll down on the ground. What was she doing wasting time thinking about the past when she had so much work to do in the here and now? Applejack gathered up the fiddles and stacked them neatly in the corner. They'd actually be useful in the next hoedown, which was scheduled for that very weekend. That is, if they won the Best in Equestria Award. Otherwise, Applejack doubted she'd be in the mood to party.

"Granny, I'd love to stay here all night, but I have to get to work," Applejack said, throwing Yeehaw onto her back.

"Got it! Just help me down," Granny Smith exclaimed, reaching out a shaky hoof. When her head popped back out, there was a weathered brown book in her mouth. "I thought you might get some good use out of this old thing." Granny wiped the dust away from the cover. The chocolate-colored leather looked like it had seen better days. There were a few apple juice stains on the back, and the pages inside were yellowed at the edges. But it was sturdy, bulky, and not unlike the journal she shared with her friends. It was actually pretty neat!

"What's this?" Applejack asked. She had never seen it before.

"It was your mother's when she was yer age," Granny explained. "For a while, the little sugarcube used to carry it around the orchard, drawing pictures of everything in sight! Until she found somethin' else to fascinate her. I think after that she was interested in bird-watching…"

It was her mother's! Applejack's heart began to beat faster as she lifted the cover. Sure enough, the first dozen pages were filled with doodles and drawings. There were sketches of everything from apple trees to old rickety fences, and a farm dog that looked a lot like Winona. Applejack turned the page. There was a drawing of a much younger-looking

Granny Smith. Applejack recognized her from all the old family pictures. It was like opening a little family time capsule.

"But I'm not much of an artist...." Applejack thought back to art class at the Ponyville Schoolhouse. The teacher, Pastel Palette, had told Applejack that the painting she'd done of her favourite tree was "amazing." Applejack could tell when ponies were being honest, and she knew the painting was awful! It was no big deal, though – Applejack knew she had plenty of other talents.

"I know, dear. I thought you could write in there." Granny smiled. "Writing is good for gettin' thoughts outta the old apple cart before they weigh ya down too much." She pointed her hoof to her head. "Trust me, you don't want all that rattlin' around up there."

"Thanks, Granny Smith." It was a nice gesture, but Applejack didn't really have time to be sitting around writing in a book when she had a whole farm to run – no matter how good writing in it might make her feel.

Applejack gave Granny a hug and headed to her room to put the treasures away. She tucked the book and Yeehaw safely under her bed. It was best to keep special things like them out of harm's way. Also best to keep 'em in a place where they couldn't distract her for now. There was no time to get lost in daydreams about fillyhood. She had a lot to do. The first thing on the list was tucking her little sister into bed; the second was victory for Sweet Apple Acres.

CHAPTER 5

Buck Up

The next morning, the air outside was as crisp as one of Applejack's prized Jonagolds. It was the ideal weather for the big job they had on their hooves, so Applejack was already feeling very lucky. She was ready to make today count. If they wanted to win the award for Best Orchard in Equestria, it was going to take a solid week of hard work. Hooves-in-dirt, muzzles-to-the-grindstone work.

Applejack had spent all night planning it out. Sweet Apple Acres was going to get a full overhaul before Blue Ribbon came to see it for himself at the end of the week. A comprehensive inventory of every tree and its average apple output, a full fix-up of the barn, and a new paint job for the sign out front. Winning would mean so much for their family – not just glory for the Apple legacy, but it'd bring in loads of new business to boot. And the extra plot of land? Well, Applejack already had about twenty different ideas for it.

"OK, Apples!" Applejack hollered with a smile. "Let's get to it!"

"All riiiight!" Apple Bloom cheered. She jumped as high into the air as her short filly legs could take her. She really loved a challenge, especially if it included helping her older siblings with all the grown-up farmwork.

"I'd save some of that energy if I were you, sugarcube." Applejack tipped her hat. "Gonna be a long day. You ready to go, Big Mac?"

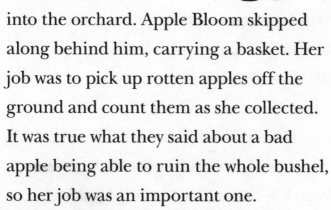

"Eeyup!" Big Mac hooked himself to a cart and took off into the orchard. Apple Bloom skipped along behind him, carrying a basket. Her job was to pick up rotten apples off the ground and count them as she collected. It was true what they said about a bad apple being able to ruin the whole bushel, so her job was an important one.

"Found one already!" Applejack could hear Apple Bloom shouting.

"That's nice, dear," said Granny as she headed back into the house. She was going to work on the books and ledgers to see how much money the farm had brought in over the past year. Applejack wanted to leave no stone unturned and no apple tree unbucked, just in case Blue Ribbon asked.

Applejack was about to get to work on her part of the orchard when she saw a pink blur bouncing in the distance. Applejack shielded her eyes from the sun. It was Pinkie Pie! How had she forgotten that today was Pinkie's day to help out with the inventory?

"Howdy, Pinkie!" Applejack shouted. Even though she knew Pinkie was horrible at bucking apples, Applejack was glad to have her friend join her. Maybe if it worked out, Pinkie would stay and help for more than one day.

"Are you ready for the best apple tree inventory eveeeeer?!" Pinkie squealed as she came to a full stop, just a few inches from Applejack's face. Now *here* was a pony who never ran low on energy.

"You bet yer cutie mark," Applejack said. "Thanks for comin'. All of us here at Sweet Apple Acres appreciate yer help."

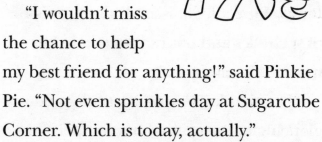

"I wouldn't miss the chance to help my best friend for anything!" said Pinkie Pie. "Not even sprinkles day at Sugarcube Corner. Which is today, actually."

"Come again?" Applejack cocked an eyebrow. She glanced at the rows upon rows of unbucked trees and thought of the precious seconds ticking by. If they started within the next three minutes, they could probably make it to the South Field by lunchtime, and then after lunch they could go to the East Field…

"It's the day when Mrs. Cake gets the new shipment of sprinkles in and has me taste all the new flavors," Pinkie Pie said matter-of-factly. "It's pretty much the best day at work ever. But I would miss a hundred sprinkles days if you needed me to, Applejack. It's what friends are for!" Pinkie Pie took out a small silver canister of sprinkles and poured some into her mouth. "Want some?"

"No, thanks," Applejack said anxiously, glancing at the sundial out of the corner of her eye. A tiny sliver of shadow made its way across the plate.

"More for me." Pinkie shrugged. She

poured some sprinkles in her mouth. "So, what's up, A.J.?"

"What's up is the sun!" Applejack exclaimed. "Which means we're already behind schedule! Follow me."

After leading Pinkie over to the first tree in a row, Applejack used all her strength to kick her hind legs out against the trunk of the tree. Twelve apples fell into the basket. One fell onto the ground. "Oh, no, you don't!" Applejack said to the apple, picking it up and tossing it in with the others. No apples were getting away on Applejack's watch. "Got that, Pinkie? A thirteen-apple yield from old Steffan here! Not bad for him." Applejack patted the trunk of the tree and looked up at its strong branches in admiration.

"Steffan – thirteen! Got it!" Pinkie Pie nodded and made a check mark on her

clipboard. "This is fuu-uuun!" She bounded over to the next tree in the line, her curly pink tail springing up and down.

"Glad you finally came around to buckin', Pinkie Pie," Applejack said. She'd always thought it was fun and hoped other ponies would see it, too. As fellow Earth ponies, she and Pinkie were perfectly suited for the job with their super pony strength. Applejack trotted to the next tree and repeated the familiar motion. Ten apples fell into the basket. Easy as pie. "Ten for Big Jim here!"

"Ten-a-roony for Big Jimmy-Jazz!" Pinkie smiled and scribbled down the number. Then she frowned. "Hmmm..."

"What is it?" Applejack said.

Pinkie scratched her head. "That doesn't seem right…"

"What doesn't seem right?"

"Maybe I have this wrong…" Pinkie frantically flipped through the pages of her clipboard. "Buuuut…"

"Pinkie Pie!" Applejack shouted. "What's the matter?!"

Pinkie started talking very fast. "If my calculations are correct, Big Jim here should have been up by at least two apples since last quarter. But instead, his yield went down by four. While Steffan did make up for this discrepancy with his extra three apples, we are still down by approximately one apple and have only surveyed precisely two trees!" Pinkie Pie sure knew a lot about an apple orchard for a gal who didn't normally work on a farm. Sometimes, Pinkie's random knowledge could catch a pony off guard.

"Well, it's lucky I don't make a habit out of countin' chickens before they've hatched or countin' apples before they've been bucked," Applejack said. "Let's just keep moving. We still have a lot of trees to go." She gestured at the orchard. The neat rows of trees extended into the distance. At this rate, it was going to take them a whole month to do the calculations, and they only had 'til the end of the week! Applejack felt her forehead begin to get sweaty under the brim of her hat. *Oh no*, she thought, *not the apple sweats!*

"OK!" Pinkie Pie said brightly. She skipped off to the next tree. A moment later, she got distracted. "Hey, Applejack?"

"Yes, Pinkie Pie?" Applejack hoisted a

bushel of apples onto her back.

"Which of these apples are going to become pies? I want to buck those first."

"Really?" Applejack rolled her eyes. It didn't matter which apples got bucked first, so long as they all did. "I suppose that'd be the Honeycrisp or the Pink Ladies...though I've made many a Jonagold pie in my day..."

"Ooooooh, interesting," Pinkie said. She nodded her head at the tree and scribbled something down on her clipboard. "You know so much about apples, Applejack."

"Well, I should hope so!" Applejack snorted. "Kinda comes with the territory of running an apple farm and all."

Pinkie's eyes grew wide. "I bet you know *almost* everything!"

"*Almost?!* I reckon I do know

everything." Applejack puffed up.

Pinkie smiled and leaned in close. "Oh yeah? What's the first ingredient you need if you wish to make an apple pie from scratch?"

Applejack didn't see how any of this was relevant, but she played along. "Well, apples fer starters…then flour, sugar, then some cinnamon…"

"No, silly, the first step is inventing the UNIVERSE!" Pinkie laughed. Then she frowned and put her hoof to her chin. "Or was it Equestria? I can't remember the *actual* words, but I read that in one of Twilight's science books. Somepony named Cart Bacon—"

Applejack reached out and put her hoof over Pinkie's mouth. "That's very fascinatin', but put a cork in it, OK!"

"Mmmmf hmp ummm smmmrf!" Pinkie Pie said, nodding.

Applejack sighed. It was tough enough to run a whole farm with a focused worker like Big Mac beside her. How was she expected to get all her work done when she had such a hyperactive pony like Pinkie Pie holding her back? *I'll make it work somehow,* she thought as she cantered over to another tree.

"Yeehaw!" Applejack shouted, and kicked her back legs with the force of ten regular ponies. Apples rained down into the baskets below. It was hard work being an Apple and a good friend at the same time, but luckily she was up for both jobs. At least she hoped so.

Chapter 6

A Day Late and a Bit Short

The golden delicious sun was starting to set over Sweet Apple Acres. "Well, butter my flank and call me a bread roll!" Applejack said as she carted the last bushels to the barn and plopped down onto the soft hay. "I'm mighty tired."

Pinkie joined in, and the two of them

looked over at the tons of apples they'd collected that day. Soon the fresh loot would have to be washed and checked again for rotten apples and sneaky worms. Then they'd be separated and shipped across Equestria in the form of delicious pies or barrels of apple juice, or just as healthy, crispy apples, the closest to perfection a piece of fruit could get.

"That's because you didn't have sprinkle power." Pinkie Pie shrugged. She bit into a fresh apple. "I hope you – I mean *we*," Pinkie Pie said with a wink. "I hope *we* win the award for Best Orchard in Equestria!" Ever since Pinkie Pie had discovered she was possibly a distant relative of the Apple family, she'd taken to referring to herself as one of them. It didn't matter if it was true or not because Pinkie thought it was lots of fun.

"That all depends on how we did." Applejack looked down at the clipboard. They had taken an inventory of only half the trees she'd scheduled for today. As she looked over the results, Applejack started to get a little bit annoyed. Why, she could have done twice as much on her own! Pinkie Pie had slowed her way down with her constant jabbering. The whole farm was now very behind schedule. This was bad. Very bad. So much for 'sprinkle power.'

"Hey, Applejack!" Pinkie said, interrupting Applejack's thoughts again.

"Hold on." Applejack frowned. Were these numbers really correct? How had the haul been so small? According to her *Equestrian Farmers' Almanac*, this season's weather had been spot-on. Applejack was sure that Best of Equestria wouldn't be impressed with this.

All of a sudden, Pinkie Pie started skipping around the barn singing: *"Oh, I've been workin' on the aaapple faaarm, all the livelong daaaaay! I've been workin' on the apple farm; it's just as fun as plaaay! Can't you hear Winona barking, sneaking up in the rows of corn? Can't you hear A.J. shouting, 'Pinkie, blow your flügelhooooooooorn'?"* Pinkie Pie whipped out her crystal flügelhorn and began blowing a series of loud honks.

"PINKIE!" Applejack gritted her teeth. "Why don't you run on home now? I think I can take the rest from here."

"Are you sure?" Pinkie Pie stopped in her tracks. "If you want, I can come back tomorrow, too. Even though it's frosting day at Sugarcube Corner, I wouldn't mind helping you finish getting ready for the big day!" She took out a small tub of purple frosting, smeared some on an apple, and then chomped down on it.

"No!" Applejack answered quickly. "What I mean is … I wouldn't want you to miss any more of the fun stuff at Sugarcube Corner. I think Rainbow Dash will help me plenty."

"Yes, Applejack!" Pinkie Pie saluted Applejack and skipped off toward Ponyville. As she bounced off into the distance, Applejack could still hear the distinctive toots of the flügelhorn and Pinkie's high-pitched singing voice.

Applejack was stressed out. She had more work to do than time to do it! She looked around the barn at all the bushels of apples. She'd done this job a million times before. Of course she'd pull it off! It wasn't about how fast they could buck all the apples and catalogue them; it was about doing a thorough, good job of it.

Remember – the trees that are slow to grow bear the best apples, she thought. *Pace yerself,* So what if Applejack had had a slow start today? That just meant that by the end of the week, she'd still have some energy to work with. She just needed to relax.

CHAPTER 7

Howdy, Journal

Applejack washed off her hooves under the barn tap and headed upstairs to her bedroom. She hung her hat on the peg and looked around the room. What now? How did a pony go about relaxing? Her eyes landed on a basket in the corner full of different-coloured wool.

"I know! I'll work on that blanket I was knittin' for Apple Bloom," Applejack announced to nopony. It was going to be the perfect relaxin' activity to take her mind off all this award hullabaloo. She chose some green yarn and found the little piece from the last time she'd worked on it. Apparently, that was a long time ago, because she could barely remember how to knit!

The more Applejack tried to loop and purl, the more the yarn became a big tangled mess. "Jumpin' jackrabbits!" Applejack exclaimed. This was the exact opposite of calming. What was she doing wrong? Was it loop, cast, stitch or loop, stitch, cast... Or neither? She scratched her head, examining the jumbled ball of yarn in front of her. Suddenly, she remembered the knitting guidebook

Twilight had given her last spring.

Applejack riffled under the bed, where she kept all her odds and ends that didn't belong anywhere else. She didn't see the knitting book, but another book caught her attention instead. It was her mother's drawing book. She hesitated for a moment, then decided to pull out the big leather tome. Applejack grabbed a quill from her bedside table and plopped down on her bed. She flipped through the pages until she found a blank page. Applejack began to write.

Howdy, Journal,

Today started like any other, I guess. Me and the other Apples got up bright and early and such. I was ready for a productive day on the farm. I had a lot of trees to buck and was excited to do it. See, I had a bee in my bonnet about how I was gonna get everything done because it's a special week. Sweet Apple Acres is up for an award – Best Orchard in Equestria! Pretty neat, huh?

Applejack stopped scribbling for a moment. She was starting to feel more relaxed already. Granny Smith was right. Applejack turned her attention back to the page and continued on:

So of course I want to win. When I told my friends about it, they kindly offered to help me get things ready around the farm. Now, I'm not one to turn down a pony who wants to work (except that one time I tried to buck all of Sweet Apple Acres on my own – but we all remember how well that turned out…), so I accepted.

Today was Pinkie Pie's turn. Don't get me wrong. I love Pinkie as much as a grub slinger loves a new spatula. But the trouble is, she's an awful farmworker! Maybe the worst I've seen. All day long, she was runnin' to and fro,

jabberin' on, and slowin' me down. If she
wasn't around, I might have gotten all my
work done. But now I'm real behind! Pinkie
Pie's 'help' was just the opposite. What a pickle.
Oh well, I guess tomorrow's a new day!

The tired pony let out a deep sigh.
Writing sure felt good. It was like all the
frustrations of the day had just left her.
Poof! Granny was right – she was gettin'
her lasso in a twist over a whole lotta
nothin'.

It hit her like a crate of apples, but all of
a sudden, the pony was plum knackered.
Applejack gingerly closed the book and put
it on the nightstand on top of the journal
she shared with her friends. She flicked off
the lamp and soon fell into a deep,
dreamless sleep.

CHAPTER 8

Leaf it to Rainbow Dash

Applejack unfurled the large scroll and laid it on the grass so everypony could see it. "All right now, Apples – *and Rainbow Dash* – here's the plan." The map of the apple farm wasn't the most attractive, but it was perfectly to scale. Applejack knew Sweet Apple Acres better than anypony, and today she meant business. She pointed her hoof at two dotted lines that snaked their way through a maze of hastily scribbled trees. She placed four tiny pony figurines that looked like game pieces on the scroll.

"I've divided the remaining sections of farm between *me*"– she pointed to the yellow dotted line and put the Applejack figurine on it – "and Big Mac." She pointed her hoof at the red line and put down a red pony figurine. "We're the team captains. Apple Bloom and Rainbow Dash – you two will be our farm-hooves. Anything we need, y'all help us with. Got it?" She smiled wide. This plan was going to work so much better than the approach they'd taken yesterday.

"Got it!" shouted Apple Bloom. The filly grinned at Rainbow Dash, enchanted by the idea that the two of them had the same assignment, probably imagining how her friend Scootaloo would be so jealous. "Farm-hooves, hoof-bump!" Apple Bloom put her hoof out to Rainbow, who didn't return the greeting.

"Uh, Rainbow Dash?" Applejack asked, eyebrows raised. "You in?"

"Ehhhh…" Rainbow Dash shrugged. She crossed her arms and leaned against a tree nonchalantly. "I don't know, A.J."

"Gotta problem, Rainbow?" Applejack asked crossly. "Then spit it out."

"The plan is *OK* and all," Rainbow Dash explained. "It's just that… I see myself as more of a lead pony than a wingpony." She shrugged.

"A lead pony?" Apple Bloom asked. "What's that?"

"At *Wonderbolt Academy*"– Rainbow Dash stuck her nose in the air –"where *I* studied, the ponies are split into teams, and then the best pony gets to be in charge." Rainbow trotted over and looked at the map. "I just think we could get all this done faster if I were the lead pony."

"Hate to break it to ya, sugarcube," Applejack said with a chuckle. "But I'm pretty sure that Sweet Apple Acres is the one place in Equestria where I am most definitely, undeniably more skilled than you."

"Eeyup," said Big Mac, nodding.

"Besides," said Applejack, leaning closer to her Pegasus friend, "you offered to help me so we could win the award, remember?"

"You do bring up a good point," Rainbow Dash conceded. She *did* want to help her friend, so her pride could be pushed aside for the day. "Can we at least get started, then? Standing around looking at this paper is boooooooring."

"Couldn't agree more!" Applejack shouted. "Everypony ready for day two? Let's make this orchard the Best in Equestria! Yeehaw!"

Hours later, Applejack was starting to feel the burn. She and Rainbow had been working their muscles all day, bucking, pulling carts, and continuing to record each tree's output. The data was essential if they wanted to prove they had the best yield of any orchard.

Applejack shaded her face and looked to the sky. She spotted a pale blue dot in the distance and followed it with her eyes. It was headed for a landing on the treetop right above her. "Apple power activaaaaaate!" Rainbow Dash shouted as she touched her hooves to the top, shaking the whole tree with all her might. The branches bowed and swayed. Three apples fell to the ground, shortly followed by a shower of leaves. Rainbow Dash flew to the ground, satisfied with the result. Applejack looked up at the naked tree. It had only a few leaves left!

"Rainbow!" Applejack reprimanded. "That's not what I had in mind when I asked you to fly to the treetops and make sure there weren't any straggler apples still hangin' on." Applejack picked up a hoof-ful of leaves and threw them up in the air for emphasis. "Just look at this!" A leaf landed on Rainbow Dash's head, and she batted it away.

"It wasn't?" Rainbow Dash said, feigning innocence. Applejack narrowed her eyes. She suspected the pony had known exactly what she was doing.

Rainbow smiled. "At least it looked awesome!"

"I want this place in tip-top shape for the Best in Equestria judges on Friday," Applejack said. "And that includes keepin' the leaves on the trees!"

"Oops." Rainbow Dash gave a nervous laugh. Her eyes darted over Applejack's shoulder. "Too late."

Applejack spun around to see that the trees behind them were almost entirely missing their leaves, too! It looked like the dead of winter, not early fall.

"Think of it this way, Applejack"– Rainbow put her arm around her buddy – "I did you a major favor. Now only the strongest leaves are left. Survival of the leafiest!" Rainbow scratched under her chin and narrowed her eyes. "I think that famous Pegasus Darwing said that—"

"I don't care if Princess Celestia said it! Just stop ruinin' the trees and help me,

please?" Applejack trotted over to her map of the orchard. She moved the tiny figurines of herself and Rainbow around. "All right, I think the

West Field needs some attention. Big Mac and Apple Bloom should be finishin' up their assigned route by now." She looked off into the distance but couldn't see anything. She thought she saw a beige pony trot between the trees and hide. Who was that? She blinked a few times and looked again. Her tired eyes must have been playin' tricks on her.

"How about I go check on them?" Rainbow Dash grabbed the action figure of herself and held it up high. She made a series of sound effects as she brought the blue pony action figure back down to the map by twisting it into a barrel roll of death. "I'll be faaaast!"

"All right, then." Applejack nodded. Maybe it would be better to work alone for a spell of time, anyway. Free of distractions —just the open fields, the fresh air, and her apples for companions. "Just be careful of the—!"

Rainbow shot off into the sky, a rainbow trail extending behind her. A tidal wave of leaves detached from their branches and billowed up in her wake. Applejack sighed and finished her sentence, "trees." Applejack was starting to remember why she had tried to buck all of Sweet Apple Acres on her own during one Applebuck season. Sometimes help was more trouble than it was worth.

CHAPTER 9

Critter Comforts

That night, Applejack curled up in bed
with her mom's book.

Howdy, Journal,

*I know I shouldn't care so much about
winning the award and such, but I do.*

*Too bad today didn't go much better than
yesterday. Rainbow Dash always has to make
such a big show of everything! Even when she's
on my turf (and supposed to be helping me),*

she acts like she's the biggest toad in the puddle. She was flying all over the place, shaking the leaves off the trees. Then when I asked her to help me buck she did the job so fast she missed half the apples! It just really chaps my leathers.

First, Pinkie was too slow, and now Rainbow Dash was too fast! Can't any of my friends get it right? Honestly...

P.S. Don't even get me started on Big Mac. I found out he chose yesterday of all days to give Apple Bloom a bucking lesson. They bucked a total of ten trees – the whole day! Why am I the only pony around here who knows what hard work is?

Outside her bedroom window, the morning sun was just beginning to peep over the horizon. A rooster began to crow,

and Applejack knew it was time to get up
and get going. There were only a few days
left to make sure things were perfect
before Blue Ribbon arrived. Applejack
yawned and closed the leather journal that
still lay open on her bed.

"Up and at 'em, Winona," she said as
she roused the sleepy
pup from her wicker
basket in the corner.
"Let's see if we can
make today any better
than the last two." Winona barked and
wagged her tail in response. At least the
dog listened to Applejack.

After a quick breakfast of warm oats
and apple jam, Applejack was ready to go.
She trotted outside and saw that
Fluttershy and Rarity were already waiting
for her. *Whoo-ee!* She had a good feeling

about these two ponies. "Howdy, girls!"

"Hello, darling," Rarity said. "How's the farm overhaul going? Well? You've already done most of the *hard* labour, I  presume?" She looked hopeful.

Applejack didn't want to tell them how awful it had been going. It would just start the day off on a bad hoof. "We made a good start, but we still got a ways to go."

"Oh, pooey." Rarity jutted her bottom lip out. "I didn't dress for hard labour." She smoothed down the fabric on the fancy getup she was wearing. Applejack thought it was silly that Rarity had worn her best clothes for a day of farmwork.

"Good morning, Applejack," Fluttershy

said. "Winona, you're looking well." The dog barked happily. Winona, like all animals, loved Fluttershy. She ran over and nuzzled against the yellow pony's legs. Fluttershy petted her and cooed, "You're a good little puppy-wuppy, yes, you are! Who's the best farm dog in Ponyville? It's you!"

"All right, you two," Applejack said, interrupting Fluttershy's puppy time. "Listen up! Now, I won't be able to keep as close of an eye on ya as Pinkie and Rainbow because I've got to finish buckin' and takin' inventory of the North Field. There was a bit of a...hitch in the schedule." Applejack considered her words carefully. She didn't want to say anything too bad about her friends and how much of a disappointment they'd been. Those thoughts could go safely in

the diary, that way nopony ever had to
hear them.

"Please, Mr. Squirrel," begged Fluttershy
in her tiny voice. "Please come on out of
that tree for Applejack! Just for a little bit.
She said that she'd be delighted to have
you back home in a few days. But—" The
squirrel hugged the tree branch even
tighter. Fluttershy frowned. "Oh well, all
right, then. I guess you don't have to."

Fluttershy trotted over to the next tree.
"Um, hello, critters. If there are any of
you in there, would you please consider
maybe coming with me for a little while?
See, my friend Applejack needs the
orchard to look just perfect and—"

"How's the critter cleanin' comin'?"

said Applejack, trotting up to Fluttershy. Applejack's hooves were caked with mud, and her yellow mane was stuck to her forehead, which was slick with sweat.

"Um, OK," said Fluttershy. She looked down at the dirt. Applejack could tell Fluttershy was lying when she avoided eye contact. "It's going great…ish."

"You know the judges won't like it if the trees aren't up to standards," Applejack said. She looked up at a squirrel. "I just don't think it'd send the right message havin' a bunch of animals up there."

"But these little guys aren't harming anypony," Fluttershy pleaded.

Applejack sighed. Fluttershy's tender

heart was getting in the way again. "Have you convinced *any* of the critters to leave?"

"A couple!" exclaimed Fluttershy. She pointed her hoof over at Winona and Angel Bunny.

"Our pets do not count, Fluttershy," Applejack said. She threw her hooves into the air in exasperation. "I give up! Why don't you go see if Big Mac needs any help in the barn?" Fluttershy nodded and trotted off. Angel Bunny and a few squirrels followed the yellow pony.

"I think I need my journal, Winona," Applejack said to her dog. But instead of hearing a familiar bark in response, she was met with silence. Winona was in the distance, chasing after Fluttershy.

CHAPTER 10

Rarity's Vision

Howdy, Journal,

*Everypony is getting on my last nerve.
I thought Fluttershy had developed a backbone
by now, but boy, was I wrong! Let's just say
that if you want somepony who will spend all
morning lettin' baby squirrels walk all over her
instead of helping out a friend, Fluttershy is
your gal. If you want my honest opinion,
I wish she woulda just stayed at home.*

Applejack slammed the journal shut and headed downstairs to get back to work. She ought to go check on Rarity's progress with the new Apple Juice Booth sign's paint job. When Applejack had gone over the list of tasks that morning, Rarity had jumped at the chance to work on it. Applejack figured it was bound to be good, considering Rarity had such an eye for design. She couldn't buck a tree to save her hide, but that pony could make anything look mighty nice.

When she arrived at the front gate, there was a big piece of shimmery purple fabric covering the sign, and no Rarity in sight. Where had that pony gone off to now? "Rarity?" Applejack called out. She thought she heard the sound of hooves behind her, so she turned around. But there was nopony there. Very strange.

"Rarity! Apple Bloom!" Applejack trotted toward the house. "Come on out and show me the new sign!"

The door swung open, and Rarity trotted out. "Sorry, darling. Granny Smith was just showing me how to get paint out of satin. It would have been *très* tragic if I'd let it dry. This ensemble would have been ruined! Can you imagine anything worse?"

"Just barely," said Applejack, picturing Blue Ribbon frowning at her and telling her she'd lost the award. Rarity was so ridiculous! What kind of pony would wear a fancy outfit to help her friend on a farm? A pony who didn't plan on doing any work at all, that's who. Applejack was about to say something mean, but she bit her tongue. "Sure glad ya didn't have to go through that," she said instead.

"You have *no* idea," said Rarity, completely missing the sarcasm in Applejack's voice. She flipped her mane back elegantly. "I'm just glad I was able to finish the sign before the incident. Do you want to see it?"

"Course I do!" Applejack smiled. Maybe she was jumping to conclusions a little too much. Rarity hadn't let her down at all.

Ugh, Journal!
     Rarity is just as bad as the rest of 'em! When she finally got around to showing me the Apple Juice Booth sign, I couldn't believe what

I saw. It was all glittery and nothin' like I'd asked for. Maybe if she spent less time thinking about her precious outfits and more time payin' attention to what her friends actually like, she'd have noticed that I hate all that frilly filly stuff! But now time is running out, so I can't even fix it. Blue Ribbon will be here to judge Sweet Apple Acres tomorrow. I guess my fate is in his hooves. At least I almost finished bucking all the trees. . .

CHAPTER 11

A Close Call

Applejack scribbled in the journal so hard that her quill broke through the page. It was just so good to vent!

Twilight just came by the farm to see if she could 'help out.' I was so busy tryin' to finish up that I didn't even want her help. I mean, look at how much all my other friends 'helped' – not at all!

Anyway, Twilight tried to suggest something

about asking the folks at Best of Equestria for
more time. She said she might be able to help
make it happen on account of bein' a princess
and all. Twilight never uses her royalty for
special treatment, so the fact that she even
mentioned it made me pretty mad. Can't she see
that if ya win by special circumstances, then it's
not really winnin'? I thought Twilight was
better than—

Suddenly, Applejack heard the sound
of hoofsteps outside her door. "A.J.?" a
muffled voice called out. "Are you up
here?" It was Twilight! Applejack looked
around, frantic for somewhere to hide the
journal. There was no way she'd want
Twilight to see any of it. Especially the
latest entry. She wouldn't want Twilight's
feelings to be hurt.

"Yeah!" Applejack called out. "Just a
second!" She put the book under the

covers, but it left an awkward square lump underneath. It was too suspicious.

"Can I come in?" Twilight asked from outside the door. "I just wanted to say"– Applejack gave up and tossed the journal under her bed with all her other junk. She ran to the door and opened it before Twilight finished her sentence – "that I'm sorry. I know how important schedules are to you and Sweet Apple Acres. Without them, you Apples would probably have a very hard time running such a successful farm!" Twilight smiled. "Hey, were you…writing?"

Applejack froze. "How did you know?"

"Your quill is on the bed." Twilight Sparkle shrugged. "Were you writing in our journal?"

"Um, I was writing in a journal." Applejack said.

"You work too hard, A.J." Twilight Sparkle put her arm around Applejack and led her out of the room. "Why don't you come and eat? Granny Smith invited us all for dinner." Applejack felt a sudden pang of guilt. She had just  written some stuff complaining about Twilight, and here she was bein' all kind.

"That sounds swell," Applejack replied. "I'm so hungry I could eat a whole bushel of apples on my own."

"I think you might just be in the right place for that," Twilight said. Applejack laughed. It felt good. Better than writing in any silly journal.

Chapter 12

The Switcheroo

Applejack hardly slept a wink. She was so nervous about the big day ahead that it felt like she'd had forty-two little butterflies flying around inside her stomach all night long. She kept imagining small tasks she'd forgotten to do or messes she hadn't cleaned up yet.

By the time the early morning rolled around, she decided to just get up instead of waiting for the rooster to crow. There was still time left to make everything perfect.

After Applejack scrubbed the barn door, fixed the gate's squeaky hinges, and tidied up the mud pit, the sunlight was just starting to hit her beautiful home. It looked glorious. The morning light crawled over the hills like fresh golden honey, slowly making everything sparkle. Applejack just happened to be standing right in front of the apple juice booth.

The brand-new sign shone brilliantly.

Every sparkle on every letter in the words *Sweet Apple Acres* stood out like dewdrops on a bushel of Honeycrisps. It was unlike anything she'd ever seen. Rarity had been right to add all those little touches. Applejack began to feel bad for being so cross about it yesterday. The more she thought of the sign, the more she realized how wrong she'd been about most of her friends this week.

The cowpony resolved to thank them all when they arrived for the judging ceremony a little bit later. They'd all done their best to help out a friend despite her not being so friendly to them in return. She was a very lucky pony.

The Apple family was all lined up outside the barn and ready to go. They were waiting for Blue Ribbon. He was due to arrive at any moment. "Great job this week, Apples!" Applejack said, hoping the encouragement wasn't too late. "Y'all worked real hard, and I just want you to know how much I love and appreciate ya. Whether we win the award or not."

"We love you, too, Applejack," said Granny Smith.

"Eeyup," nodded Big Mac.

"Where's yer friends, sis?" asked Apple Bloom. She craned to see if anypony was coming down the lane. "Didn't they say they were all comin' to the judgin'?"

"They did say that…" Applejack bit her lip in concern. Her little sister had a point. Pinkie Pie, Rainbow Dash, Fluttershy, Rarity, and Twilight Sparkle should have shown up a long time ago. Something strange was definitely going on, but she couldn't focus on it right now. All she could do was wait for Blue Ribbon.

"Hey, Applejack! I almost forgot," Apple Bloom said. "I did somethin' else to help you out last night!" She looked proud of herself.

"You did?" Applejack smiled. "And what was that?"

"I heard Rainbow Dash sayin' she wanted to write in the journal, so I found it in yer room and gave it to her."

"You what?!" Applejack's heart dropped into her stomach. Had Apple Bloom accidentally given Rainbow Dash the wrong journal? The two did look similar. Brown leather, about the same size... "Where did you find it?"

Apple Bloom continued, "It was under yer bed with Yeehaw!" Applejack didn't wait to hear the rest. She darted into the house and took the stairs four at a time. She threw open her bedroom door and dived under her bed. She riffled through the junk until she saw a brown leather book. *Please be the right one*, she prayed.

She reached for the journal and flipped it open. Inside, she saw an entry about Cranky Doodle Donkey.

Applejack's heart sank. Rainbow Dash had her private diary – the one where she'd written all those horrible things about all her friends!

Now it made perfect sense why they hadn't shown up. Maybe it was a good thing she still had the group journal, because Applejack certainly felt like she had just learned a whole new, very important lesson about friendship.

Chapter 13

In the First Place

A giant rainbow arched toward Sweet Apple Acres. "Aaaah!" screamed Blue Ribbon as he ducked for cover. Applejack stayed where she was. She knew that Rainbow Dash was just putting on a show. But what was she doing here after all the things Applejack had written about her?

"Hey, dude," Rainbow said, landing about an inch from Blue Ribbon. He cowered in horror. "How's it going? You checking out this awesome farm or what?" Applejack was gobsmacked. What in tarnation was going on?

"Uh, Mr. Ribbon—" Applejack started, but she was overpowered by a high-pitched squeal.

"Wooo-hoooo!" shrieked Pinkie Pie, bounding over to them. "Are you ready for the best farm-judging inspection thingy eveeeer?!" She passed him a balloon in the shape of an apple.

"Have you seen the gorgeous new sign yet?" Rarity asked, prancing up to the befuddled judge. "It was *all* me." Rainbow Dash shot her a look. "Ahem . . . by 'all me,' I of course mean myself and the incredible Apple family!"

"I'm really sorry about the squirrels," Fluttershy said to Blue Ribbon. "The little sweeties just love it here so much, they can't imagine being anywhere else. It's so *lovely* here. All the nice fresh air and yummy apples and—"

"All right, guys. I think we can take it down just a notch," said Twilight Sparkle. "Let the stallion do his thing." She nodded at Blue Ribbon. "Apologies, sir. Please, continue..."

"Right. Thank you." He handed his apple balloon to Apple Bloom and got out a clipboard and a quill. He looked over the papers Granny Smith had given him about the farm's yield. He nodded his head in approval. "Most impressive, Apple family. Now all there is left is for you to show me your orchard and facilities. Young stallion, would you care to take me on a tour?"

"Eeyup," said Big Mac.

"Do you ever say anything else?" Blue Ribbon asked.

"Nope," replied Big Mac as they turned the corner and walked through the orchard, out of sight.

Applejack let out a giant sigh and looked to her friends. She studied their faces. When a couple of seconds ticked by and nothing happened, she couldn't help it anymore. "Did y'all read my journal or not?!" Applejack blurted out in despair.

"Yeah..." said Rainbow Dash nonchalantly. "Well, technically only *I* did...out loud. To them." She pointed her hoof at the four other ponies.

"If it makes you feel any better…" said Fluttershy. She looked down at the ground. "I didn't want to hear it."

"None of us did," Twilight said. Her face was serious.

"I didn't really think the one about me was too bad." Rarity shrugged. "Luna knows, there are *way* more embarrassing things in my diary." Rarity shuddered, remembering when Sweetie Belle had leaked some of it to the school newspaper's gossip column. "At least all of Ponyville didn't read yours."

"So hold up"– Applejack brightened –"you mean to tell me y'all aren't mad at me? You still want to be my friends even after all those terrible

things I said?" She looked around.

"Well, I'm not sure…" Pinkie Pie finally said. "Some of that stuff you wrote wasn't very nice…"

Applejack deflated. But then Pinkie giggled. "…but I liked the part where you compared me to a spatula, so I guess we're good."

"Thank you, Pinkie," Applejack said, tearing up. At least she still had one friend left. "I'm sorry, everypony. I hope y'all can find it in yer hearts to forgive me." She started to pace back and forth in front of them. "See, honesty is not just my Element of Harmony, it's the pony I am. When I try to hide it, I just don't feel right," Applejack admitted. "When I was writin' all those nasty things, I wasn't bein' honest with myself. Which is to say, I was bein' a huge jerk and letting my own ambitions get in the way of the most important thing – my friendship with all of you."

"Uh, Applejack?" said Rainbow Dash with a smirk.

"Yeah?" Applejack lifted her chin up to Rainbow.

"We totally already *know* all that," she said like it was nothing. "And *of course* we're still your friends! It takes more than some silly words in a journal to get rid of us. Right, everypony?" Her friends murmured their agreement, laughing. Applejack felt so grateful. It was like winning the best award she could ever dream of. She didn't even care about the prize anymore. All she needed to be happy were her family and friends. And that was the honest-to-goodness truth.

Chapter 14

Sweet Apple Success

Applejack still couldn't believe they'd won the Best Orchard in Equestria award! It turned out that Blue Ribbon had been secretly stopping by the orchard all week long, watching them work! He'd seen Applejack and her friends (who were clearly inexperienced farmers) banding together to work the land. He was so inspired that he felt he had to give them the prize. It was the extra-special something he was looking for – a farm that not only had exemplary apple yield numbers, but one that was willing to teach ponies new skills.

The blue ribbon stamp looked mighty fine on the Sweet Apple Acres crates that had been shipped out to Canterlot Castle, and the new prized plot of land was starting to look more like a fledgling orchard every day.

Applejack leaned back in her lounge chair and watched the scene unfold. If

any of the new farm-student ponies had any questions at all, she knew they'd come to her.

Otherwise, she was going to sit back, relax, and enjoy the view: a beautiful piece of land and ponies of all kinds coming together to farm on it.

Off in the distance, Fluttershy and Scootaloo were listening to Apple Bloom give a lesson on proper bucking form. To the left, Lyra and Pinkie Pie were having a heated discussion to determine whether trees should be planted twenty or twenty-seven hooves apart. And Rarity was talking to Aloe about the possibility of planting the trees in a heart-shaped pattern instead of traditional rows so the orchard could be admired by the Pegasus ponies up in Cloudsdale as well. Applejack never knew there could be so many new and creative ideas for farming.

"Hey, Applejack?" Twilight Sparkle said as she trotted up.

"Yes, Twilight?" Applejack replied. "Ya need some help with those Gala seeds?" She jumped out of her lounge chair eagerly.

"No, no. Sit back down, silly." Twilight smiled. "I just wanted to ask how this month's Applejack's Honest Farming Advice column is coming along. It's so cool that Blue Ribbon wanted you to take that on!"

"I know," said Applejack. "I just hope I'm doing an OK job of it."

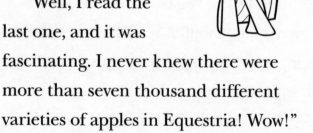

"Well, I read the last one, and it was fascinating. I never knew there were more than seven thousand different varieties of apples in Equestria! Wow!"

"Sure are! And new hybrids are bein'

invented all the time." Applejack blushed and looked down at the scroll on her lap. "Shucks, I never thought I'd be the one teachin' you things, Twilight."

"You know so much about all of this." Twilight gestured to the field. "And once you're done with them, so will all the ponies across Equestria!"

Read on for a sneak peek
of the next exciting
My Little Pony adventure,

Fluttershy and the Furry Friends Fair

The local park was a haven of respite and peaceful relaxation for the residents of Ponyville. The leafy trees and little hills covered in soft green grass were perfect for stretching out one's wings, reading a book, or just looking at the clouds above and daydreaming about what shapes the Pegasi in Cloudsdale might make next.

A sweet yellow Pegasus pony named Fluttershy lived on the outskirts of town and loved to trot through the park every single day. It was nice to take a break from her busy job as a caretaker of animals, big and small. When she went on her walks, Fluttershy liked to reflect on her life and think about how lucky she was that it was one filled with fun, furry critters and friends.

One day, as she strolled along on her normal route, Fluttershy noticed that something was different about Ponyville Park. There was a jaunty melody echoing across the grass, through the hedges, over the knolls, and under the shade of the tall oaks. It sounded like it was coming from the area near Froggy Bottom Bogg. Though Fluttershy had every intention of ignoring the distraction, her pet bunny, Angel, went hopping off toward the noise.

"Oh, OK, Angel," whispered the meek yellow Pegasus. Angel Bunny had

Fluttershy wrapped around his furry little paw. It was hard for her to say no to such an adorable face.

"Let's go see what that commotion is, you curious little dear." Fluttershy brushed her soft pink mane away from her left eye, spread her wings, and flew after him. "I'm sure it won't take long."

In truth, Fluttershy *actually* wanted to go home for a cup of dandelion tea and a nap with her new litter of kittens, but she wasn't going to ruin Angel's fun. He was only a young bunny and needed plenty of new experiences to grow – in addition to healthy food and weekly tail fluffings. Fluttershy had noticed that lately Angel had been very curious about all the "hoppenings" in Ponyville. Just today, Fluttershy had taken him by the Ponyville Schoolhouse to visit the fillies and colts during playtime. Then they'd gone to the market to see if there were any cherries for sale, and finally to Sugarcube Corner for a special bunny carrot cupcake made by Pinkie Pie. A busy day by anybunny's standards.

Angel arched his head back to marvel at the sight. *What's this, Fluttershy?* his big eyes said. The yellow pony had a special connection with all her animals. She almost always knew exactly what they were trying to convey, whether they could use their voices to tell her or not. Angel was particularly unique, though. Fluttershy could look into his eyes and just know what he was trying to tell her. Most of the time, anyway. Sometimes it took a few guesses.

"I'm not sure what's inside, Angel, but I think I've seen it before..." Fluttershy replied. The tent in front of them was definitely familiar. It had red and white vertical stripes with a big top in the middle. The triangular yellow flags at the top had the symbol of two hats side by side. Fluttershy scrunched up her nose in polite distaste. It was those swindlers the Flim Flam brothers again! They weren't very nice ponies.

"We don't want to go in there," Fluttershy said, looking down at Angel. "Do we, sweetie?" Flim and Flam had made a business out of creating fake get-well tonics and tasteless apple juice. They were always looking for the next cheap way to make money from unsuspecting ponies.

I want to see! Angel hopped up and down excitedly and forged ahead to get a closer look at the two framed posters near the entrance. FARNUM AND FAILEY PRESENT THE TOP HAT BUNNY CABARET, they said in big, bubbly letters. A picture of a brown rabbit with very long fur was in the middle. He was wearing a red bow tie and sitting on a black top hat. There was a flag in his paw that said FEATURING THE MOST TALENTED BUNNIES IN EQUESTRIA (PLUS FROGS). RABBITS & RIBBITS!

Angel pointed his paw at the poster and smiled. *Can we go inside?*

"Well, that's not what I was expecting at all." Fluttershy giggled. "I suppose if anything can get my attention, it's cute bunnies."

Angel turned to her and crossed his arms with a pout. Suddenly, he didn't like the idea of Fluttershy paying more attention to other bunnies than to him.

"Don't worry, little love. You're *my* top bunny!" Fluttershy patted Angel on his downy head and purchased two tickets for the show.

Inside the tent, there was a flurry of preshow activity. Ponies were taking their seats on the wooden benches, buying refreshments to munch on (the popcorn came in a novelty cardboard top hat), and chatting about what sorts of amazing bunny tricks they were about to behold. Fluttershy had never seen so many ponies excited about bunnies in one place. She was in great company.

Angel led the way to the front row and took a seat right in the middle. He clearly didn't want to miss a single hop or nose twitch of the performance. "Do you want some carrot juice, Angel?" Fluttershy asked, gesturing to the refreshment stand. She always tried to make sure her pets stayed hydrated.

The little white rabbit shook his head defiantly and pointed his paw at the seat next to him.

"Not even just a sip or two?" Fluttershy replied hopefully. Angel stuck his nose in the air. Then he pointed to the seat again. Fluttershy obeyed and sat down. What a convincing little fellow he was!

As the rest of the audience found their seats, Fluttershy petted Angel's soft white ears and smiled. This was a nice treat for the two of them. Maybe if the show was really entertaining, she would bring some of the birds and squirrels by tomorrow for a field trip. Or Toby the fruit bat. Toby *did* love a good cabaret.

The jaunty music began to play again, and a tiny marching band of bunnies entered the stage wearing blue costumes with sparkling gold accents, each playing a different instrument. Leading the way was a large black rabbit with white spots playing a tuba. *Honk, honk. Honk, honk.* The bunnies hopped into formation, and a moment later, two tall yellow stallions danced onstage. They had short red manes and wore black tuxedos and top hats. One of them had a red moustache. They each had a frog on his shoulder.

"I'm Farnuuuum!" sang Flim, extending a hoof out to the right.

"And I'm Faaaailey!" added Flam, reaching his hoof to the left.

"Welcome to the Top Hat Bunny Cabaret – exciting entertainment on the DAILY!" They danced around each other in time to the music. "We bet you've never laid your EYES, on bunnies like these little GUYS!"

"You're in for a treat!" Flim shouted.

"You're in for a PRIZE!" Flam warbled. "The Top Hat Bunny Cabaret! Ponies, what d'ya saaay?!" Flam put his hoof to his ear as if he were listening.

"OK!" the ponies in the crowd shouted.

"Hooray!" shouted Flim in response.

"Because we've got Fuzzy Lops and Himalayans, Hot-de-Trots – know what we're sayin'?" Flim and Flam turned to the bunnies and patted each one on the head as they sang, *"Golden Palomino or Harlequin, whichever you like – we're nonpartisan!"*

Flam took off his top hat, waved a wand around, and then pulled out a light purple rabbit wearing sunglasses. The rabbit began to juggle three golden orbs while hopping on one foot. The audience clapped and cheered. "See? This one can juggle balls!"

"That one can hop up walls!" Flim shouted, pointing to a long-haired grey bunny hopping sideways up the wall of the tent.

"This one cooks macaroni!" A tiny spotted bunny stirred a bubbling pot and waved to the crowd. He sprinkled some cheese on the pasta and scooped up a serving for a mint-green pony named Lyra. Lyra smiled and began to gobble up the yummy food.

"That one can lift a pony!" Sure enough, a little white bunny with black spotty ears hopped over to Sea Swirl and lifted the pony high into the air. It was utterly unbelievable!

Meanwhile, the bunnies in the band

continued to play their instruments, dancing back and forth to the lyrics. On every fourth beat, one of the frogs would croak. Flim and Flam did a spin in time with each other and reached their hooves to the crowd. "So get ready to feast your EYES, on these amazing little GUYS!"

"The unsurpassable!"

"…most desirable!"

"So incredible!"

"…try *commendable*!"

Flim and Flam shuffled to the sides of the stage and held their hooves out to present the bunnies. "The *hippity-hoppity*! Ribbity-rabbity! Tippity-toppity…Top Hat Bunny Cabareeeeeeet!"

"Plus frogs!" added Flam.

"Croaaak," said his toad.

The audience erupted in excited

cheers, stomping their hooves on the ground in grand applause. Angel got up from his seat and began to hop up and down, clasping his paws together. His eyes sparkled with wonder, and a big smile was plastered on his face. Fluttershy felt all warm and fuzzy inside at his elation. There was nothing better than seeing one of her pets happy.

Read
Fluttershy and the Furry Friends Fair
to find out what happens next!

Turn the page for a
special surprise from
Applejack!

Howdy, partner,
These homegrown bonus
pages are just for you!
Have a rip-roarin' time filling
them out and sharing them
with your friends!

Your friend,
Applejack

The A-maze-ing Orchard

Applejack needs to find the best route for bucking apples in the orchard. Draw a line connecting all the trees that still have apples so she knows where to go. Make sure you lead her to the basket at the end so she can bring them all back to the barn in time!

My Special Somethin'

When Granny Smith is looking for something in the attic, she finds Applejack's old toy pony, Yeehaw. Applejack feels happy remembering all the fun times she and Yeehaw shared together. Do you have a favourite extra-special toy? What does it look like? Does it have a name? Use the space below to draw your special somethin', and write what makes it so much fun!

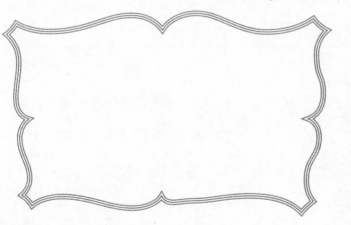

My toy's name is _____.

This toy is the best because it's _____,

_____, and _____.

I got this toy from _____.

Sweet Apple Searchin'

Applejack needs all the help she can get if she's going to win the prize for Best Orchard in Equestria. Can you help her by finding these missing words? The words might be in any direction.

P	P	Y	R	L	J	G	J	R	B
I	S	I	O	A	P	P	L	E	R
E	P	R	I	Z	E	Z	Q	R	B
E	A	R	T	H	P	O	N	Y	T
B	L	U	E	R	I	B	B	O	N
W	K	B	Q	P	R	E	N	I	C
C	C	Y	N	O	P	W	O	C	W
C	U	E	P	S	W	E	E	T	V
H	B	S	D	N	E	I	R	F	P
V	O	R	C	H	A	R	D	G	C

**APPLE   BLUE RIBBON   BUCK
COWPONY   EARTH PONY
FRIENDS   ORCHARD   PIE
PRIZE   SWEET**

One Bad Apple

One bad apple can ruin a whole bushel! Draw an X through the rotten apples in this barrel. Then, when you've found them all, count them. Record your total below.

Total:
_____

Howdy, Journal
part 1

Until her friends started a group journal to record their friendship lessons, Applejack had no idea how much she loved writing! Even though her own journal got her into a little bit of a pickle, she still likes to write in it from time to time. Do you have a journal? Start one here by writing about your day.

_____

_____

_____

_____

_____

_____

_____

Hats Off!

Applejack may not be one for fashion, but she sure does love her trusty cowpony hat. It keeps her mane off her face and the sun out of her eyes while she works. But Rarity thinks Applejack should try some new hats for a fancy party in Canterlot. Draw different hats on Applejack and change her classic look!

Hide 'n' Seed

Pinkie Pie accidentally knocked over Applejack's seed crate! Now the packets are all mixed up. Help her sort them out by matching the seed packets on the left with the labelled crates on the right.

In First Place

When Sweet Apple Acres wins the award for Best Orchard in Equestria, part of the prize is a very special ribbon. Blue Ribbon needs your help designing the one to give to Applejack and her family. Put your own flair on the blank ribbons below. Then choose your favorite to give to Applejack!

Flavourful Fruits and Veggies

If there is anything ponies love to eat (other than cupcakes!), it's lots of fresh fruits and veggies. In fact, the Apple family grows more than just apples. They have all sorts of fresh treats on the farm, like carrots and celery. What veggies do you like? Use the log below to record all the fruits and veggies you eat this week. Put a star next to your favorite ones — two stars if it's something you've never tried before!

Day	Fruits and Veggies	This Was Yummy!
Monday		
Tuesday		
Wednesday		
Thursday		
Friday		
Saturday		
Sunday		

My favourite fruit was _____.

My favourite vegetable was _____.

Howdy, Journal
part 2: family

Applejack considers herself a lucky pony because she has such a fun and loving family. She especially loves spending time with her big brother, Big McIntosh, and little sister, Apple Bloom. Her siblings can get on her nerves sometimes, but they are mostly a lot of fun! Do you have siblings? What are they like? Describe them here. If you don't have any, write about a friend who feels like a brother or sister.

Shady Characters

Applejack will never forget the time she brought Bloomberg, one of her beloved trees, on the train to Appleloosa. Even though he has a good home now, she still misses him because she loves each and every tree in the orchard. Is there a tree in your garden or the park that you like? Maybe its branches provided shade for you on a hot summer day or perhaps they are perfect for climbing. Draw a picture of that particular tree below.

Hoofprints

Use the space below to have your family and friends sign their autographs, write you a note, or even draw a little picture. Looks like Applejack has already made her mark!